BULLETS AND BREAD

FAITH AS ARMOR

BY

BILAL YASIN

About the Author

Bilal was born in Yabrud, Palestine, where hardship and faith shaped his early life. At seventeen, he came to America determined to build a better future. His journey led him through dangerous neighborhoods, relentless obstacles, and a devastating government investigation that tested his strength, dignity, and hope.

Today, Bilal shares his story as a reminder that no matter how hard life becomes, perseverance and faith can carry a person through even the darkest storms.

Dedication

I dedicated the book. To my Mom, Dad, and my family.
Which is my kids.

Acknowledgement

Though the challenges often felt impossible to recover from, Bilal refused to give up. His resilience was fueled by gratitude to God and the unwavering support of his wife, and the motivation he received from Arthur, Joyce, White, and Kevin Jones.

Table of Contents

About the Author...ii

Dedication..iii

Acknowledgement...iv

Chapter 1 Before the Fall...1

Chapter 2 The Road to Chincas..5

Chapter 3 Earning My Place...8

Chapter 4 The Camera on the Pole....................................12

Chapter 5 The Camera in the Sky......................................18

Chapter 6 Judged by Labels, Defined by Actions.............28

Chapter 7 The Weight of Accusation.................................33

Chapter 8 Still Standing: What Faith Builds After
Everything Falls Apart..39

Chapter 1
Before the Fall

I was born in 1969, in a modest village named Yabrud, nestled in the hills of Palestine. My early years were spent in a household that knew hardship as intimately as it knew family. I was raised alongside my two brothers and three sisters, although one of my sisters was born later and didn't grow up with us in the same home. Life in Yabrud was simple and often harsh. Opportunities were scarce, and dreams rarely stretched beyond the boundaries of survival.

In 1973, when I was just four years old, my father made the courageous decision to leave for the United States in search of a better future for our family. His younger brother, already living in California, helped him with the paperwork and the transition.

My father worked tirelessly, sending money back home so we could survive. Life under Israeli occupation was difficult, resources were limited, movement was restricted, and dignity often felt like a luxury. The dream of a freer, more hopeful life always seemed far away.

At the age of 17, in 1986, that dream began to take shape for me. My father had filed the paperwork for me to join him in the United States, and I arrived in California full of hope, ambition, and a belief in the promise of the so-called American Dream. Like so many others, I believed this was the land of "milk and honey." Everyone said so. Freedom, opportunity, and the chance for a better future — these were the ideas I carried with me as I stepped onto American soil.

When I arrived, my father was living in Concord, California, and I stayed with him. Within my first week, I found a job as a busboy at Sizzler Steakhouse. I didn't have a car, so I commuted on a bicycle. The job paid enough to cover my rent and food. It was exactly what I had come for: an honest chance to work and make a living.

It's interesting how I got my first job. I rode my bike up and down the street, looking for work. I applied at a Sizzler Steakhouse, but they didn't call me back. After three days, I decided to call them myself. When I spoke to the manager, he asked why I was calling. I told him I was following up on my application. He replied, "We get 60 or 70 applications, and people expect us to call them, but we don't like doing that. Since you're calling yourself, you must really need the job. Why don't you come in tomorrow?"

I went in the next day. The manager looked through the stack of applications and pulled mine out. He told me that because I had called, it showed that I really needed the job, unlike others who just filled out the forms and waited. Thank God, he gave me the job. I started the next day, wiping tables, cleaning bathrooms, and washing dishes. Sizzler was a busy steakhouse, but I was grateful to be working.

I worked at Sizzler for about five to six months. At the same time, I also worked at a local liquor store from 6 p.m. to 11 p.m., stocking the cooler with beer, wine, and soda, and cleaning the floors. One job wasn't enough, so I had to work both. But the double shifts quickly wore me down. I remember standing in the cooler, the cold air biting my skin, dozing off while holding a case of beer. After about a week of this, I realized I couldn't keep going — it was simply too much. So I quit the liquor store job, but I continued at Sizzler until I joined my father in his business.

Not long after, I moved from Concord to Stockton, California, where I stayed for roughly a year, from early 1987 until almost the end of 1988. My father and uncle had purchased a gas station with a small grocery store, and I worked there during that time. Stockton had a reputation — a rough, unforgiving place where newcomers were tested — and I quickly found out why.

In my first months there, gangs began coming into the store. They weren't customers; they were there to size me up. Their message was clear: This is our territory. They wanted to intimidate and control the business, the way they had done with others before me. I refused to be controlled.

They began with what we called "beer runs" — two or three of them would swagger in, grab beer and other drinks, and sprint for the door without paying. The first few times, I let it go. The fourth or fifth time, I decided it was enough. As they bolted for the door, I chased them, heart pounding, baseball bat in hand. I caught one in the back with a swing and, in the heat of the moment, kicked their car door hard enough to dent it before they sped away.

Two days later, they came back, and this time they were ready. They pulled the same stunt, but when I stepped outside with the bat, one of them pressed a gun against my head and fired a shot into the air. The sharp crack echoed through my ears. My heart felt like it had stopped, but my body kept moving as he forced me back inside, the cold metal still against my temple.

"Open the register," he demanded. I refused. He tried to do it himself, one hand holding the gun, the other fumbling at the till. In that split-second, instinct took over, and I grabbed the gun. We wrestled, shoving and twisting, each trying to point the barrel away from ourselves. Time slowed to a crawl. My mind was racing: If I let go, I'm dead.

Then another man came around the counter. I didn't see the punch until it landed, a sharp, exploding pain to my temple that sent me sprawling. Through ringing ears, I heard him yell, "Shoot him! Finish him!" The gunman pulled the trigger — click. The gun had jammed. "It's jammed!" he shouted in frustration. I knew then that God had spared me.

Shaken, I opened the register. They grabbed the cash and fled into the night, leaving me standing there, breathless, staring at the dented counter and the silent gun.

Chapter 2
The Road to Chincas

After leaving Stockton, I began traveling with my father, who was a vendor selling Native American jewelry, handcrafted silver, and turquoise bracelets, earrings, and rings. He sourced them from artisans in New Mexico and sold them across the western states, from California to Montana. I traveled with him for about two and a half years, eventually getting my own car and my own product line. But the constant travel worried my mother. She didn't want me living out of a car, moving from state to state. She wanted me to settle down.

In 1992, I moved to Chincas, California. With the help of my uncle, we bought a small grocery store called Chinkas Market from a local family. My father and uncle handled the purchase, and I managed it, opening and closing the store every day.

At first, it was just me and an older woman named Sarah who had worked there under the previous owners. She stayed on for six to seven months part-time before retiring. After she left, I was mostly alone until 1994, when my younger brother immigrated to the U.S. and joined me in running the store. We also had a kind-hearted employee named Alberto who worked with us for a time before he passed away. May he rest in peace.

But Chincas, like Stockton, had its own dangers. The market sat in a neighborhood with four or five different gangs, white, Black, Mexican, Norteño, Sureño, and even some Oriental and Native groups. Each had its own colors, codes, and turf boundaries, and none liked the idea of an outsider owning a business in their territory.

From my first week, I could feel the tension. They'd hang around the parking lot, watching. Testing me. Sometimes it was just words; other times, it was more. There were fights in the aisles. Guns drawn. Bullets slamming into the front windows at night. I was shot at maybe eight or ten times, not counting the robberies, holdups, or the times a cold barrel was pressed against my face during an argument gone wrong.

The police became a regular sight. Sometimes they came every day, sometimes every other day, responding to yet another 911 call. For nearly two years, this was the rhythm of my life, open the store in the morning, navigate the unspoken politics of gang territory during the day, and pray to make it through the night without trouble.

It took time — years, really to prove that I wasn't leaving, that I could be trusted, that I wasn't there to challenge anyone's pride. Slowly, grudgingly, the tension eased. The market became more than just a place to buy groceries; it became neutral ground, a spot where everyone, no matter their colors or affiliations, could come without fear.

It was a hard-won peace, but it allowed me to plant my roots. I got married, started a family, and began to build a stable life in Chincas. From the dusty roads of Yabrud to the aisles of Chinkas Market, the journey had been anything but easy — but it had been mine.

Chapter 3
Earning My Place

When I first came to Chincas, it felt like I was walking into Stockton all over again. Different streets, different faces, but the same struggle. The neighborhood had its own order, divided among groups: white, Black, Mexican, North Indian, Sureños, and Asian crews. Each one guarded its space fiercely, determined to run the block their way.

For someone like me, a newcomer trying to build a business in the middle of their territory, it was dangerous from the start. They didn't want me there. They didn't trust me. To them, I was just another outsider who thought he could set up shop and make money in their backyard.

The first years were chaos. I had guns shoved in my face, fights in and outside the store, robberies, bullets shattering the night, and punching holes in the walls. Those walls still carry scars, small jagged holes that tell the story better than I ever could. More than once, I thought I wouldn't survive.

I can't even count how many times I had to dive for cover, ten, maybe more. I got shot at, held up, beaten down, and yet every morning I opened that shop again.

The police knew my address by heart. They showed up almost every other day, sirens flashing, answering another 911 call. For nearly two years, that was my normal life, living under siege, surviving one day at a time.

But eventually, something began to shift. People started to see that I wasn't going anywhere. I wasn't afraid, and I wasn't there to judge or interfere. Slowly, faces that once glared at me began to nod in recognition. Some even smiled. The store, once a target, became part of the rhythm of the block, a corner everyone passed by, a sign that had always been there.

One afternoon, I was sweeping the sidewalk when a police cruiser rolled up. A tall officer stepped out, boots crunching on gravel.

"Afternoon, Officer," I said, brushing the dust from my hands. "Did I do something wrong?"

He shook his head, smiling faintly. "No, not at all. I just wanted to check on you. I haven't heard from you in a month, month and a half. Usually, I'm stopping by every other day because you've had some sort of trouble. I figured something might've happened."

I didn't know whether to laugh or feel sad. Trouble had been so constant that my silence now worried him.

"Well," I said, "thank you for coming by. And thank God it only took two years for people to finally accept me, to trust me, to let me simply be here."

He nodded, though I could see he remembered those nights too, sirens wailing, fists pounding on the counter, the sound of shots echoing in the dark.

And just like that, life in Chincas began to calm. The store was no longer a battleground but a meeting place.

People came not just to buy, but to talk, to share a laugh, to show respect. For the first time, there was a sense of peace.

But peace never lasts long. A new kind of pressure began to creep in, not from the streets, but from the law.

"Bilal," they would say, "you know everybody. You know the gangs. You know who's selling drugs. You could really help us out."

They came to me ten, maybe fifteen times. Police, sheriffs, CHP, parole officers, and even task forces. Each time, the request was the same: give us names, tell us who's moving what, be our eyes and ears.

But I couldn't. I wouldn't. Because in neighborhoods like mine, the word "snitch" isn't just an insult, it's a death sentence.

I tried to explain. "These people are my customers. What am I supposed to do? Ask everyone who comes in, 'Are you in a gang? Are you selling dope? Are you using?' And then tell them they can't buy a soda or a bag of chips? That's not my job. My job is to run the store, to treat people with respect, whether they're wearing work boots or gang colors."

Still, the pressure didn't stop. Each time I said no, I could feel their suspicion harden. It was as if refusing to help them made me guilty, like I must be hiding something. Their stares lingered too long, their questions dug too deep, and the weight of their doubt hung in the air like smoke.

The gangs once saw me as the outsider, but now it was the police who made me feel like I didn't belong.

In the end, I chose survival. I refused to betray the people who had finally accepted me, because I knew the price of betrayal. If I snitched, I wouldn't last a week. Someone would be waiting in the shadows, finger on the trigger.

So I told the officers the same thing, again and again:

"Find your own way. Get your own people. I'm not here to work for you."

Because my only job was to keep the doors open, keep my head down, and make it through another day alive.

Chapter 4
The Camera on the Pole

Back then, I wasn't even at Chinca's most days. My grind was wholesale, Yasin Distribution, driving case to case, supplying smoke shops and corner stores with accessories. That detail mattered later, when people swore I was right in the middle of everything. The truth was, I was on the road, trying to keep the lights on.

It started with a box.

One morning, a big metal box showed up across the street, bolted to the top of a telephone pole, about a foot wide, two feet long, aimed squarely at our parking lot and front door. At first, a branch spoiled the view. By the next day, someone had trimmed that branch clean. Now the lens could see everybody and everything.

I noticed it, frowned, and went back to stocking shelves. But customers noticed too, and they weren't quiet.

"Bilal, what's that box?"

"Is that a camera?"

"Why's it pointed at your door?"

Questions turned into suspicion. Suspicion turned into lost sales. One man told me flat out, "I don't know what you're up to, Bilal, but I'm not coming back."

The store wasn't a market anymore. It was an exhibit. People parked further away, pulled caps low, and avoided us altogether. You can measure that kind of fear on a register tape. The numbers dropped and kept dropping.

I called everyone. Chincas Police. Sheriff. CHP. Nobody claimed it. Finally, I called the FBI in Sacramento. The woman on the line said no, too.

"Okay," I told her, "if no one owns it, I'll cover it myself with a ladder and a garbage bag."

That's when she stopped me. "Wait, wait. Actually, yes —it's ours. We're looking for a fugitive. We were told he comes into your store."

The next day, agents walked in with a photograph of a man none of us had ever seen. "That's why the camera's there," they said. It never felt true. It felt like a story told because I wouldn't stop asking.

Then came Avarice. She spoke Spanish, carried herself like she wore three badges at once—FBI, Homeland, ABC. With her, the lines between agencies blurred into one shadow. The message was simple: we're watching you.

The box stayed. My business bled. And on February 3, 2005, they made their move.

They took me in front of my own market, 1406 Boucher, hands cuffed, and hustled me into a white van. One agent wore a uniform top, the other a vest that looked like armor. They read me my rights. The one who said the FBI flashed a badge and laid down the rules: tell the truth or face five years. Then came the questions about money, about Hamas, about mosque attendance, about "brothers." Another agent pressed on cigarettes and marijuana, warning I could lose the store if I didn't cooperate. The FBI asked me outright if I would work for them.

Figure 1: Local newspaper coverage of the undercover sting and arrest (2005).

They searched my home. They took my computer, discs, Arabic letters to my wife from her family, around $14,000 in cash, my father's rifle, and my van. The ledger of a life, seized in one sweep.

I denied what wasn't true. I told them over and over that I had never sent money to any terrorist group.

Inside the Courtroom

Two years later, I sat in a Superior Court courtroom in Butte County. The wood-paneled walls, the American flag behind the judge's bench, the sound of the reporter's fingers snapping across the machine—those details are burned into me.

Judge Steven J. Howell leaned forward. "Mr. Yasin, before you testify, you must understand that anything you say can be used against you if this motion to dismiss is denied."

My attorney, Mr. Denny Forland, turned to me. "Do you understand that?"

I nodded. "Yes. I still wish to testify."

The prosecutor, Mr. Jennings, folded his hands. "Nothing further, Your Honor."

The questioning began.

"Where were you born?" Forland asked.

"I was born in Palestine."

I told the story of my family, my brothers and sisters, and the small businesses I built. I told them about Yasin Distribution, about knowing nearly every convenience store owner in Butte County, about being the only Palestinian, the only Muslim among them. I spoke of my mosque on Nord Avenue, of praying less than I should but still holding faith.

Then the cross-examinations began.

The prosecutor objected often. "Nonresponsive, Your Honor."

"Sustained," Judge Howell said more than once.

When I spoke about the arrest in the van, Jennings objected to hearsay. My attorney pushed back, "Not offered for the truth, Your Honor, only to show what was said."

This time, the judge allowed it. I testified about the FBI agent who told me there was $80,000 in my house, who accused me of sending money to Hamas, and who threatened to seize everything unless I confessed.

The courtroom grew tense when I described the camera. I told them I had photographed it myself a week after the arrest. That picture—Defense Exhibit J—was shown to me. "Yes, that's mine."

Later, it was renumbered as Exhibit L after a mix-up with other exhibits. The judge ordered older procedural exhibits to be relabeled AA, BB, and CC to avoid confusion. Even the paperwork seemed to twist and turn.

I described how the FBI later returned some of my property under a May 3, 2006 order: the computer, the disks, the family letters. They handed me two checks totaling $14,000. But not everything came back. The van was gone. My father's rifle was gone. He still missed it.

"Do you believe you've received all of your property back?" Jennings asked on cross.

"No," I said. "Maybe ninety percent. But not my van. Not the rifle. Some money is still missing."

The Battle Over Discovery

When the evidence was done, the lawyers shifted to argument.

Mr. Foster, co-counsel for my co-defendant, stood and told the court: "The FBI instigated this case. Yet they have not turned over the discovery showing why they began investigating Mr. Yasin. That omission is fatal. We ask for dismissal."

Mr. Forland joined. Mr. Ortner, representing Cabrera, joined too. All three defense lawyers spoke with one voice: the government had hidden the reason the camera went up in the first place.

Mr. Jennings responded carefully. "Your Honor, the People submit that the only issue before the court is whether dismissal is warranted solely on the discovery issue. We contend it is not."

Judge Howell rubbed his chin. "I will take the matter under submission. I will issue a written ruling. We will reconvene in two weeks."

The gavel fell. The case, and my life, hung in the air.

That's how it happened. Not just the box on the pole, not just the lost business, not just the van and rifle they never gave back. But the courtroom too the objections, the exhibits, the questions about Hamas, about 9/11, about brothers who were only brothers in faith.

If you've never lived under suspicion, you don't know how it stains. It doesn't shout. It whispers. It turns family letters into exhibits, greetings into investigations, and prayers into evidence.

People ask when the investigation began. They want a date, a case number. I tell them it began when I looked up and saw a branch had been cut to give a camera a better view of my door.

From that moment on, I wasn't being watched because of what I did. I was being watched because of who they thought I was.

And once they write a story about you, the truth has to fight for every sentence.

Chapter 5
The Camera in the Sky

It all began with a quiet shift, a new view from across the street. The FBI had put up a camera, bolted it to a telephone pole right in front of my store. But when it was first set up, a tree blocked the view. Only about 80% of the parking lot and storefront were visible. I could sense that wasn't enough. They wanted a clear, uninterrupted view—a total surveillance of everything around the store.

So, they hired landscapers. These workers weren't there to cut down the entire tree. They just trimmed the branches that were blocking the camera's view of the lot. And sure enough, the next day, the camera was fully exposed. It was about two feet by one foot, bolted high up, aiming directly at my front door.

It wasn't just the camera that changed things; it was the atmosphere that followed. The customers noticed. They'd come in, their eyes darting to the camera, then glancing over their shoulders. Many asked, "Bilal, what's that? Is that a camera? Why's it pointed right at your door?"

At first, I brushed it off, but the suspicion in their voices was impossible to ignore. Some refused to come inside at all. They parked farther away, or they didn't stop by at all. It became clear I was losing customers. Every day, a little more. Sales dropped steadily, and I could measure it in the emptiness of the register tape.

I called everyone I could. The Chincas Police. The Sheriff. Highway Patrol. But no one knew anything. Everyone said, "Not us." Finally, I called the FBI in Sacramento, desperate for some clarity.

"Do you have anything to do with this camera?" I asked.

"No," they said.

"Well," I replied, "If no one owns it, I'm going to take care of it myself. I'll get a ladder, wrap it up with a plastic bag, and cover it so my customers don't feel like they're being watched."

That's when the woman on the other end of the line stopped me.

"Wait," she said. "Actually, yes, it's ours. We're looking for a fugitive. We've been told he comes into your store."

The next day, an FBI agent showed up while I wasn't there. My employee, who was working at the time, said the agent handed him a picture of a Hispanic man and asked if he recognized him.

"No," my employee said.

The agent then told him, "We've got a camera on the pole because we're looking for this man."

That was their explanation. And just like that, the story seemed to fit, at least on the surface. The agent's visit made it seem like they were simply trying to catch a fugitive.

When I returned, my employee told me what had happened. But the whole thing still felt like a thin excuse, a lie meant to explain the surveillance.

But we accepted it, grudgingly. The camera remained, and so did the questions. Even with the agent's explanation, people kept coming in, asking about the camera. "Oh, they're looking for a Mexican guy," they said. "They're looking for him, that's why the camera's there." But the discomfort never went away.

Days turned into weeks. Then came Avarice.

She was an undercover agent, speaking fluent Spanish and carrying the weight of every government agency you could imagine—FBI, Homeland Security, ABC. Her presence felt heavy, like she had authority without explanation. She made it clear that they were watching us. Watching me.

A few days after her initial visit, Avarice began making a routine of stopping by the store. She'd come in and speak to one of my employees, who had limited English but spoke fluent Spanish. She presented herself as a woman in need, claiming to be broke, traveling from Sacramento, and needing money for gas. The story seemed innocent enough at first.

But her true intentions soon became clearer.

Avarice started by asking to buy cigarettes. She presented a receipt for the cigarettes, claiming she couldn't get any cash from her credit card. She purchased two cartons of cigarettes, offering them at a significantly lower price than retail. My employee, feeling sympathy for her story, agreed to buy them from her.

But this wasn't the end of it. Avarice continued to come back. Each time, she purchased more cigarettes. Each time, the amount she bought grew, and so did the pressure.

After a few visits, she started hinting at wanting something more. She asked my employee if he knew where to get drugs, cocaine, heroin, or crack. She pressured him, her intentions now clear. This wasn't about cigarettes anymore; she was trying to draw him into something far darker.

She didn't get what she wanted. My employee wasn't involved in any of that. So, Avarice moved on, trying to set up a deal that would involve more than just cigarettes.

The deal she proposed this time was even bigger—she offered to sell five to ten cases of cigarettes, each case containing 30 cartons. She asked for $12 per carton, a deal too good to resist. But then, she made her real demand. She wanted drugs in exchange for the cigarettes.

I couldn't believe it. She was pushing him to get involved in something illegal, something dangerous. And she wasn't letting up. She said if he couldn't help her, she wouldn't bring the cigarettes at all.

I thought about it. If I had the drugs she wanted, I would have acted quickly, no hesitation. But I didn't. I told her, "I can't help you with that, but I can buy the cigarettes from you." She wasn't interested in that. It was clear that she wanted something else.

But then the pressure grew. She came back again, asking for marijuana this time. She seemed to lower her expectations, asking only for a small amount, something I could possibly supply. It was a slippery slope, but I still didn't have the drugs she was asking for.

She kept pushing.

And then, one day, the moment came. She showed up with a van full of cigarettes, about 10 or 12 cases, and the deal went through. I paid her in cash. The cigarettes were supposedly legit, bought from a large wholesaler, not stolen. But it didn't matter. The FBI, Homeland Security, ABC, and a full SWAT team were already on the scene. The camera, the surveillance, it had all been building up to this moment.

I handed over the money and received the cigarettes, but no sooner had I made the exchange than the doors burst open. The SWAT team, dressed in full riot gear, rushed in, guns drawn. They arrested everyone.

Figure 2: News photographs from the undercover operation and arrests.

I was cuffed and thrown into the van. As I sat there, still processing what had just happened, the FBI agents started their interrogation. One of them, Porter, began asking questions.

"How much money did you send to Osama Bin Laden?" he asked.

"How much money did you send to Zarqawi? Hamas? What do you think about September 11th? We expect to find over $80,000 at your house. How much do you have there?"

I answered them. I denied it all. "Osama Bin Laden doesn't need my money," I said. "I don't know what you're talking about."

But the questions didn't stop. The FBI had already made their decision. The case was built. And now, it was my turn to defend myself, to prove I was innocent of the things they had accused me of.

It felt like I was up against a wall, a never-ending cycle that only tightened with every step. My case was pushed forward to the 9th Circuit Court, but the moment it reached the appeal court, my heart sank. The judges rejected the chance to even hear my case. Their reasoning was simple: the statute of limitations had passed. It was like they'd thrown the clock in my face, counting down until I was unable to hold the government accountable for what they had done to me.

I had planned on suing for a civil rights violation, hoping for justice in a system I thought was meant to protect people like me. But the government had an answer to that. Their one weapon, the statute of limitations, was dragged out deliberately, it seemed, until it was too late. They had used time against me, knowing that the more they stalled, the more likely I'd miss my chance to fight back. They knew exactly what they were doing.

Two years, four months, almost two and a half years had passed. Every day that dragged on felt like another nail in the coffin of my fight for justice. The court postponed hearings over and over, and each delay cost me more, more stress, more money I didn't have, and more hope slipping through my fingers. I showed up, month after month, for at least 30 court dates, knowing I was losing everything. But I couldn't stop. There had to be justice, didn't there?

Each time I walked into that courtroom, I could feel the weight of the world bearing down on me. The uncertainty, the helplessness. It wasn't just a case anymore; it was my life on the line. And yet, every time, I walked out with nothing.

The frustration grew. With every passing month, I found myself sinking deeper into debt, taking loans to pay for my attorney, my expenses. I had no choice but to keep moving forward, hoping for a miracle. In my heart, I still believed in justice. How could I not? It had to come, right? The system was supposed to protect the innocent, wasn't it?

But as the months wore on, the reality hit harder. The government, cold and calculating, knew exactly what they was doing. They weren't worried about justice. They weren't worried about what was right. They were worried about protecting their own interests.

I kept thinking about insurance. When a car accident happens, you're covered. If you hit someone, you pay for the damage. Even if you're at fault, you make it right. But the government? They had the biggest insurance in the world, their power—and yet they used it to crush me. They could have paid me back for what they took. Instead, they left me to suffer in silence.

I felt like a train had run me over, then they just walked away, leaving me in the wreckage. The government didn't even offer the decency of a proper apology. No, they simply let the time run out, knowing full well that the statute of limitations would stop me from holding them accountable.

And all the while, I lost everything. My business, my property, my home. I watched it all slip away as I fought a losing battle. I'd offered to sell my land, my business, anything to keep up. But even that was a fading hope.

In the back of my mind, I couldn't let go of the idea of getting justice. I would send letters to the justice department, desperately hoping someone would care. I even imagined myself walking to Washington, D.C., taking my papers to the Capitol, screaming for justice. But I didn't have the means to do it. My car was falling apart, uninsured, and unregistered. I couldn't even get my kids to school without worrying about getting pulled over by the police.

I remember a time when I was pulled over. My heart sank as I saw the flashing lights behind me. For two and a half years, I had been driving with no insurance, no registration. Every day, I dodged the law just to keep moving. And now, I had finally been caught.

I sat in the car, sobbing, overwhelmed by everything that had happened. It wasn't just the fear of being caught; it was the sheer weight of everything that had come crashing down on me. I didn't even know how I started crying. It just poured out.

The officer came to my window. He asked me if I was okay, and I couldn't even answer him at first. He recognized me, though. He knew me as the man from Kington's Market —the man who had been wronged by the government. "Are you the guy from Kington's?" he asked. "What happened to you with the FBI?"

I nodded, still choking on my tears. He looked at me and saw the pain in my eyes, the struggle I was going through. And then, in an unexpected moment of kindness, he told me, "I'm going to act like I never saw you, brother. Just go home. Pick up your kids. Get out of here."

It was a moment of grace in the midst of chaos, a moment that reminded me that, despite everything, there were still good people in the world.

But that didn't change the reality. The government had already taken everything. They seized my van, my money, and the letters from my wife's family. Letters that were worth more than anything in the world to me. They combed through every part of my life, taking anything they could get their hands on. The computers, the hard disks, everything.

A year and a half later, the FBI returned some of my property. They gave me back my computer, the letters, but not the things that truly mattered. My van was gone, my cash was gone. The things they took were never returned.

The more I thought about it, the more it sank in: this wasn't just a mistake. This wasn't just a system that failed me. This was fraud. They had done this intentionally. They had used the statute of limitations as a weapon, knowing they could drag the case out just long enough to prevent me from seeking justice.

The coldness of it all—the way they had treated me like I was nothing, like I didn't matter—made my blood boil. I had done nothing wrong. I wasn't a criminal. Yet here I was, fighting for my rights in a system that seemed designed to break me.

I kept asking myself, Why me? Was it because I was Muslim? Was that the reason they targeted me, that they tried to destroy my life? I couldn't help but think that in all of Butte County, no one had been treated like I was. None of my customers—my friends—had faced anything like this. But I had. And for what? Because of my religion? Because of my name?

That thought gnawed at me, deep and raw. The injustice was suffocating, and the feeling of being targeted, of being nothing more than a suspect in their eyes, crushed me. But I kept going. I kept fighting, even though I felt like I had nothing left.

I tried to push forward. I kept telling myself that there had to be a way to make it right. There had to be a way to get my life back. But every time I reached out for justice, the door slammed shut. And the longer the battle went on, the harder it became to keep my head above water.

But I never stopped believing. I couldn't. For all the pain, for all the loss, I still held on to the idea of justice. Even if it seemed impossible, I would keep pushing. Because in the end, all I wanted was what was rightfully mine.

Chapter 6
Judged by Labels, Defined by Actions

Looking back at everything that happened, it still amazes me how the authorities came to see me as some kind of dangerous figure, as if I were a real threat. The scale of their response was unbelievable. You would think they were going after a terrorist mastermind. Over a hundred agents showed up. Homeland Security, the FBI, local police, and even a full SWAT team were brought in from Sacramento. I remember standing there thinking, How in the world did they reach that kind of conclusion about me? The whole thing felt completely over the top, almost like something out of a movie. But after a while, I understood. Their entire investigation was built on nothing but assumptions, fear, and ignorance.

And the sad part is, before any of this happened, my life was good. Thank God, really good. Normal. I was living the kind of life most people hope for. I was working, raising my kids, taking care of my family, supporting my wife, doing what any responsible man would do. I felt like I was living the American dream in my own simple way. I wasn't someone looking for trouble. I was just building a life. Everything was moving the way it should.

Then one day, they came for me, and everything changed.

It felt like my whole world had flipped upside down in an instant. They tore apart the life I had created. They singled me out, dragged me into a nightmare I had never imagined, and made every part of my life harder. I found myself running around trying to keep my job, keep up with school, stay close to my wife and kids, all while dealing with lawyers and trying to survive the stress.

Bills were piling up. People in the community were whispering. My reputation took a hit. Even the basic things, like keeping the electricity on, became a struggle. My life changed so completely that even the way I lived, ate, and thought was different. It was like everything got rearranged overnight, and I had no choice but to adapt.

Meanwhile, the government was spending all this time and money investigating me, a man who had committed no crime at all. A man whose only so-called crime, according to them, was being a Palestinian Muslim. Being an Arab. Somehow, those labels were enough to make them think I was dangerous. But I knew those things had nothing to do with who I was.

Still, I couldn't understand why they were so afraid of me. What did they think I had done? What did they think I was capable of? It felt like I was being punished for simply existing. Like they had already decided who I was before they ever met me. The whole investigation felt like they were trying to pull apart my identity piece by piece. They didn't care about the real me. They cared about the version of me they had made up in their heads.

One of the strangest and most personal parts of all this was the way they questioned my religion. They wanted to know how often I prayed, if I went to the mosque every morning, and if I was doing all five prayers every day. It felt like they weren't just checking facts. It felt like they were examining my soul, trying to decide whether I was a loyal American or some kind of threat.

The truth is, I am not perfect in my practice. I know that. I don't pray as often as I should. But those questions made me think. Not because of anything they thought, but because they reminded me of the kind of believer I wanted to be. When they asked if I went to the mosque in the mornings, and I told them no, it stirred something in me. It made me want to reconnect with my faith, not because of them, but because of me.

To them, the fact that I didn't go early in the morning meant I wasn't dangerous. But that shows how limited their thinking was. They made everything black and white. If you pray a lot, you're suspicious. If you pray less, you're harmless. That way of thinking is not only wrong, it's also dangerous. It ignores the real meaning of religion.

For me, being religious is about having a good heart. It's about kindness, honesty, and community. It's not about counting how many times someone prays. I have never hurt anyone. I have never wronged anyone. But they couldn't see past the outside. They saw the word Muslim and immediately created a whole story around it.

Eventually, I came to understand just how deeply they had misjudged me. Their assumptions were rooted in fear and ignorance, not facts. They let labels overshadow everything else. They painted me as a criminal when I was nowhere near one.

But even after all that, the damage was done. My reputation suffered. My finances were destroyed. Everything I had saved over the years was gone, spent on attorneys and legal fees. I went from one lawyer to another to another. Even the court transcripts cost me thousands of dollars. It felt like every step of this journey came with another hit, another weight on my shoulders. None of it was easy. None of it was fun.

Still, I refused to let those things define who I was. I focused on what mattered, my family and my responsibilities. I worked hard, paid off a huge loan even with the crushing interest, and pushed myself to rebuild. It was exhausting, but I kept going because I believed I could still make things right.

The justice system failed me. That much is clear. But I would not let that be the final chapter of my story. I realized that real justice doesn't always come from courts or institutions. Sometimes it comes from knowing the truth within yourself. I let go of revenge. I let go of wanting an apology. I put it all in God's hands.

Now, years later, I can say honestly that I have never harmed anyone. I have never allowed what happened to turn me bitter. I moved forward with faith and with love for my family. Life keeps moving, and I thank God for every day I get to live, breathe, and grow.

I trust God's plan even more now. Yes, the system failed me. But God never did. I no longer think about what they did to me. What matters is that I stayed true to myself, kept my faith, worked hard, and didn't fail my family. Life goes on, and every moment is a blessing, even the hard ones.

Chapter 7
The Weight of Accusation

From the beginning, everything that happened arrived like a storm gathering silently above me, building itself out of clouds I could not see until lightning struck. I often think back to those early days and wonder how something so devastating could begin so quietly and then explode so violently into my life.

They approached me with no clarity and no honest foundation. They suggested things that went against every belief and principle I carried in my heart. They wanted me to serve as an undercover source for them, something that would have placed my safety and my dignity beneath their interests. I refused, believing that anyone with a conscience would reject such a suggestion.

I never imagined that my refusal would mark the starting point of a long, painful journey that would change everything around me.

When they decided to come after me, they did not come like people searching for the truth. They came like people who had already decided I was guilty of something terrible. The media was already present before anyone even spoke to me. Cameras were pointed toward my home like weapons ready to fire, waiting to capture my humiliation, not any form of justice.

Figure 3: Media coverage that shaped public perception before the truth was known.

They were not interested in who I truly was. They were interested in a story, a dramatic moment, a picture worth selling. I became that picture in their minds without ever being given a voice to defend myself.

I remember sitting with the FBI investigator whose name remains burned in my memory. Even inside that van, even with my future uncertain and my rights already violated, I tried to speak calmly. I told him that what they were doing was wrong and that exposing me to the world without truth or evidence was unjust. I even offered him a way to walk away peacefully. It was not because I feared exposure.

It was because I valued my dignity. I asked him to remove his agents and remove the media, and we could end the matter there. He looked at me with a kind of amusement and told me they had more to uncover, as if my innocence itself was suspicious. At that moment, I understood that they were not searching for the truth. They were searching for something to justify the story they had already built.

They questioned how I owned my home, how I saved for it, how a working man could possibly build a life for himself. I explained that I had owned my business for almost twenty years, that I saved small amounts slowly, as any responsible person would. Instead of respecting hard work, they treated it like evidence. T

hey did not want to believe a man could achieve something honestly. They preferred to assume a crime existed because that would make their actions feel justified. They threatened to take my business, my home, and everything I built, not because I was guilty, but because they wanted to frighten me into being someone they could control.

For six long months, they investigated me quietly, secretly, watching me as if I were some dark figure hidden behind a familiar face. They allowed rumors to spread and fear to grow while they searched for anything that would support the false picture they had already painted. Yet after all that time, they found nothing because there was nothing to find. Their own prosecutors saw nothing meaningful in my case. They passed my file from one person to another like something unwanted, something embarrassing, a case nobody wished to touch.

Each time I entered the courtroom, a new face stood across from me, and every face revealed the same truth. There was no evidence, no foundation, no justification. Yet the process continued because once a machine begins to move against someone, stopping it becomes harder than starting it.

I was never shown a search warrant. Not a single signature from a judge authorizing the violations against me. I lived through the consequences while they ignored the most basic rules meant to protect innocent people. They treated the Constitution like something that applied only to others and not to them. They acted as if I were unworthy of the rights I had always respected and lived under.

One day, they came and blocked off my entire street, placing my home at the center of suspicion as if something explosive lived behind my front door. They forced neighbors away, brought in police units, dogs trained for bombs, and robots designed for emergencies. My neighbors stood outside, confused and terrified, looking at my house as if they were waiting for flames or destruction. It broke something inside me to see fear on their faces directed toward the place where my children slept. When nothing happened, when no danger was found, everything should have returned to normal, but it did not.

The damage remained.

Neighbors who once waved at me or shared small conversations began turning their heads away as if my presence threatened their safety. Some crossed the street to avoid walking near my driveway. I saw fear replace friendship, suspicion replace kindness. A person can live in a house and still feel homeless if the people around him stop seeing him as a neighbor and start seeing him as a danger.

When I went to the mosque the following day, I hoped for peace. I hoped that the place where I prayed, where I felt closest to God, would be a place of comfort. Instead, I saw groups separate when I approached. People moved away from me in silence, pretending they did not see me or hear my greetings. I felt like a stranger in the place where I came to show my devotion. It is a painful thing to stand in the house of God and feel abandoned by the people you considered part of your spiritual family.

Returning to my business only made things worse. Some customers whispered that I must have made a deal with the government. They believed I had become a snitch simply because I was back and not locked away. I was labeled first as a criminal and then as someone who betrayed his own community. Both lies, both cruel, both heavy enough to break a person.

I became a man surrounded by people but completely alone. Neighbors avoided me. Customers doubted me. Even members of my religious community feared being seen near me. The only ones who remained close were my children and God. I held on to my belief that God sees what human eyes refuse to see and that truth remains truth even when the world chooses lies.

People often asked how I survived with my mind intact and my heart still beating. They could not understand how someone could walk through so much suspicion and public humiliation and still stand upright. Many told me they would have collapsed under that weight. Some said they might have taken their own life. I heard those words with sadness because I understood how close a person can come to breaking when everyone turns their back.

But I did not break.

I kept breathing because I believed my innocence mattered. I kept standing because God never leaves a person alone, even when everyone else walks away. The pain I carried was something no one else could fully feel. People can feel sympathy, but they cannot feel the burn unless they have been in the fire themselves. Even my family felt sadness for me, but they did not carry the flame that touched my life.

Everything that happened to me must be understood not as a simple investigation but as the destruction of a life already built with sacrifice and struggle. It was an attack on my character, my reputation, and my peace of mind. It showed me how quickly the world can turn its back, how easily fear replaces compassion, how simple it is for people to believe the worst instead of asking for the truth. Through everything, I held on to faith, to dignity, and to the belief that the truth would not disappear, no matter how deeply they tried to bury it. I walked through the darkest days knowing that God was watching, even when no one else cared to see.

Chapter 8
Still Standing: What Faith Builds After Everything Falls Apart

At the end of everything, there was God.

When every door closed, when every promise failed, when the systems I trusted did not protect me, I was left with one truth that could not be taken away: my faith. I had tried, with everything in me, to seek justice through the government. I believed that if I followed the rules, told the truth, and endured patiently, fairness would eventually prevail. But it never did. Justice did not arrive. Answers never came.

There comes a moment in life when waiting becomes heavier than walking away. That moment changed me.

I stopped expecting rescue from anyone but God. I stopped asking why and began asking what now. I realized that survival itself was an act of faith. And so I placed the past behind me, not because it no longer hurt, but because carrying it was costing me my future.

The years that followed were not easy. Healing was not immediate. Stress had settled into my body, my mind, my spirit. There were nights when sleep would not come, mornings when hope felt distant, and days when simply getting through felt like an achievement.

But slowly, quietly, life began to soften again. Normality returned in small pieces, routine, work, laughter, peace. Nothing dramatic. Just progress. And sometimes, progress is the greatest miracle of all.

By the grace of God, I rebuilt my life.

I returned to work with humility and determination. I focused on what I could control: effort, honesty, and responsibility.

I worked hard, not only to survive, but to restore dignity to my life. My family depended on me. My children needed stability. My parents deserved peace of mind. Failure was not an option.

People often say, if it doesn't kill you, it makes you stronger. For me, that strength was not loud. It was not aggressive. It was quiet endurance. It was learning how to carry pain without letting it poison my heart. It was discovering that once you survive the worst, nothing else in life ever looks the same again.

Problems that once felt overwhelming became small. Fear lost its power. I had already faced the bottom—and lived.

Eventually, by God's will, I rebuilt my business. I returned to real estate. I stood back on my feet financially and emotionally. Today, I live a life that is not extravagant, but decent, stable, and honest. And after everything I lost, that feels like wealth.

But my suffering was never mine alone.

My wife stood beside me through uncertainty and fear. My children lived through years they will never get back. My parents carried worry from afar.

The hardship touched everyone I love. That reality stays with me. And now, one of my greatest purposes is to give back—to provide the comfort, security, and experiences they were denied while I was fighting for survival.

Alhamdulillah, my family is well. My wife and children are thriving. My parents are healthy and living in Palestine, and we visit them whenever we can. May God grant them long lives filled with peace and blessings. Seeing them content reminds me why endurance matters.

To anyone reading this who is walking through hardship, injustice, or loss, do not surrender to despair. I did not. Even when I had no proof that things would improve, I held onto belief. Faith is not certainty. Faith is choosing to hope when certainty is gone.

Life will test you in ways you never imagined. It will strip you down until you question your strength, your purpose, even your worth. But as long as you are breathing, your story is not finished. As long as you stand back up, you are still in the fight.

There is a truth about hitting rock bottom: once you are there, there is nowhere left to fall. The only direction is up. I reached the bottom of the bottom. And slowly—patiently—I rose again.

I rebuilt without help. I survived without justice. I endured without recognition. And through it all, God remained.

I remember where it all began—$2,000 in cash and $2,000 in credit. That was my starting point. From that small foundation, I built a life once before. And after losing almost everything, I proved to myself that I could build it again.

That is the lesson I leave behind.

Never give up. Keep your faith. Protect your family. Do not allow bitterness to define you. Time does not pause for pain, the clock keeps moving whether we are ready or not. What is lost is gone, but what remains is still yours to shape.

Life is beautiful, not because it is easy, but because it continues.

I would not wish my journey on anyone. But if my story helps even one person hold on through darkness, then every hardship had meaning.

Today, by the grace of God, my family is safe. My life is stable. My heart is at peace.

And after everything, I am still standing.